The Goodnight Star

Megan

C016092333

For Kerenza Megan, who loves the stars – A.S.

For Roland – J.M.

Amy Sparkes is donating 5% of author royalties to ICP Support, aiming for every
ICP baby to be born safely **www.icpsupport.org** Reg. charity no. 1146449

THE GOODNIGHT STAR A RED FOX BOOK 978 1 782 95368 5
Published in Great Britain by Red Fox, an imprint of Random House Children's Publishers UK
A Penguin Random House Company

Penguin
Random House
UK

This edition published 2015
1 3 5 7 9 10 8 6 4 2
Text copyright © Amy Sparkes, 2015   Illustrations copyright © Jane Massey, 2015
The right of Amy Sparkes and Jane Massey to be identified as the author and illustrator of this work has been asserted in accordance
with the Copyright, Designs and Patents Act 1988. All rights reserved. No part of this publication may be reproduced, stored in a retrieval system, or
transmitted in any form or by any means, electronic, mechanical, photocopying, recording or otherwise, without the prior permission of the publishers.
Red Fox Books are published by Random House Children's Publishers UK, 61–63 Uxbridge Road, London W5 5SA
www.**randomhousechildrens**.co.uk www.**randomhouse**.co.uk
Addresses for companies within The Random House Group Limited can be found at: www.randomhouse.co.uk/offices.htm
THE RANDOM HOUSE GROUP Limited Reg. No. 954009
A CIP catalogue record for this book is available from the British Library.
Printed in China

Penguin Random House is committed to a sustainable future for our business, our readers and our planet.
This book is made from Forest Stewardship Council® certified paper.

The Goodnight Star

Amy Sparkes ✦ Jane Massey

RED FOX

One beautiful starry night, something magical happened.
And it happened to a little girl called Megan,
who couldn't sleep because she was afraid of the dark.

Megan's room seemed full of shadowy shapes that night.
She pulled the blankets tightly around her, but still she felt afraid.

So Megan stared at the beautiful starry sky.
The stars always made her feel better.
"I *wish* I wasn't afraid of the dark,"
she whispered.

Then ... **wait!**
She thought she
saw something.
She rubbed her eyes
and looked again ...

"A shooting star!" gasped Megan.

She watched as it flew down from the sky ... past the moon ... through the clouds ...

getting closer and **closer** and **closer** and ...

Whoosh!

It zoomed through her bedroom window!

Megan chased the star's glittery trail as it twinkled
and sparkled all around the room.

"Wait, Little Star!" she laughed,
but it bounced and darted and whizzed too fast!

Then Megan had an idea. She grabbed her pillowcase,
and swoop! She caught the star!

"You're the most beautiful thing I've ever seen!" said Megan.
The shadows fell away as its soft glow lit her bedroom.
"What should I do with you?" she said as the star wriggled
in the pillowcase.

"I'd love to keep you,
but you can't fly around
in my room. Maybe I
should take you outside."

The star lit the way
as Megan quietly
crept down the stairs.

She looked out at the back garden.
"It's very dark out there, Little Star," she said.
"Stars love the night, but I'm scared of the dark."

The star bounced around happily in the pillowcase.
"All right, Little Star. I'll try."
Bravely, Megan opened the door and stepped outside.

She opened the pillowcase...

... and away the star flew!

"Wait for me!" Megan laughed, and forgetting
the darkness, she skipped after the star.

They watched the hedgehogs gather . . . and played hide-and-seek in the trees.

They stared at reflections in the pond and, lighting the garden as they went, they danced under the moon.

Once or twice, Megan even thought she glimpsed a fairy,
flitting in the starlight.
"Do you know what, Little Star?" she whispered. "I don't mind
the dark any more. Not when you're with me."

Then she noticed something sad.
The star's glow was beginning to fade.
"What's the matter, Little Star?"
asked Megan. "Are you tired?"

The star flew up a little towards the sky,
then sadly drifted back down.
And then Megan understood . . .
The star needed to go home.

"You've helped me, Little Star," said Megan. "Now it's my turn to help *you*."

Holding the star carefully, she climbed up to her treehouse in the tallest tree in the garden.

Above her, the night sky twinkled with millions of stars.
But there was a little patch of black – something was missing.
Megan knew it was time to say goodbye . . .

"Thank you, Little Star. You made my wish come true," she said. "But now you need to go back where you belong." She gave it one last cuddle, then sent it soaring into the sky.

Whoosh! Up the star flew,

going faster and faster . . . higher and higher . . .

And the faster and higher it went,
the brighter and brighter it shone . . .
until finally it found its home in the sky.
Megan smiled as she crept back to her bedroom.

From that night on, if ever Megan
felt afraid, she would look for the
one star that glowed and sparkled
brighter than all the rest.

And with her goodnight star twinkling in
the sky, she would soon be fast asleep.

Goodnight,
Megan!

Goodnight, Star!